Demi
the Dressing-Up Fairy

This is Caitlins book

Special thanks to Sue Mongredien

For Lola Jasmine Hart,
with lots of love

ORCHARD BOOKS
338 Euston Road, London NW1 3BH
Orchard Books Australia
Level 17/207 Kent Street, Sydney, NSW 2000
A Paperback Original

First published in 2011 by Orchard Books

HiT entertainment

Illustrations © Orchard Books 2011

A CIP catalogue record for this book is available
from the British Library.

ISBN 978 1 40831 294 0

5 7 9 10 8 6 4

Printed and bound in China by Imago

The paper and board used in this paperback are natural recyclable
products made from wood grown in sustainable forests. The
manufacturing processes conform to the environmental regulations
of the country of origin.

Orchard Books is a division of Hachette Children's Books,
an Hachette UK company

www.hachette.co.uk

Demi
the Dressing-Up Fairy

by Daisy Meadows

ORCHARD

The Fairyland Palace

The Orangery

The Lake

Maze

Petting Zoo

PETTING ZOO

Topiary Garden

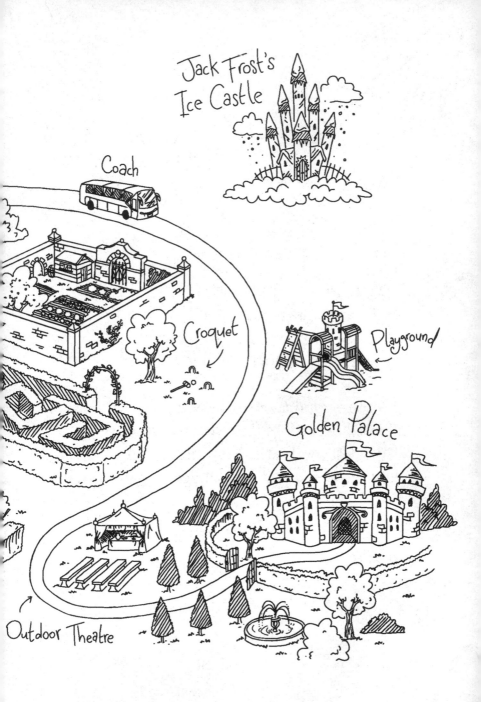

The fairies are planning a magical ball,
With guests of honour and fun for them all.
They're expecting a night full of laughter and cheer
But they'll get a shock when my goblins appear!

Adventures and treats will be things of the past
And I'll beat those troublesome fairies at last.
My iciest magic will blast through the room
And the world will be plunged into grimness
and gloom!

Contents

Cool Jewels

Kirsty and Rachel walked along the stone corridor with a group of children, all chattering excitedly. It was the second day of their holiday at Golden Palace, a beautiful stately home in the countryside, and they were having a wonderful time. Golden Palace itself was amazing – it had been built from gleaming white stone hundreds of years ago, and had high towers topped with golden turrets.

The owners of the palace were running a special 'Kids' Week' during the spring half-term, which included lots of different fun activities. Kirsty and Rachel were staying all week, and loved the fact that they were sleeping in a bedroom with a four-poster bed where real princes and princesses had once slept before them!

That wasn't the only brilliant thing about their holiday here, though. Yesterday the girls had found themselves on a brand new fairy adventure – this time, helping the Princess Fairies look for their magical tiaras. The Princess Fairies were cousins of the King and Queen of Fairyland, and had been their special guests at a Fairyland Palace ball. But naughty Jack Frost and his mischievous goblins had invited themselves to the ball

too — and had stolen the seven Princess Fairies' magical tiaras. The tiaras were full of powerful fairy magic, and without them, no human or fairy could have a happy or magical time.

"Come and see the palace's Jewel Chamber, guys," said Louis, one of the palace stewards who was looking after the children. "Through here."

Kirsty and Rachel followed the group into a small wood-panelled room, which had glass display cases arranged on the walls.

"Wow," breathed Kirsty, as she peered in at the first case. "Lady Charlotte's christening bracelet from when she was a baby — a gift from the Spanish royal family, over two hundred years ago!"

"And here's a silver helmet that a knight would have worn," Rachel said, gazing in at the next case. "This sign says it belonged to a knight called Sir Beaumont, who lived here in the eighteenth century." She grinned. "It's

so exciting to think about lords and ladies and knights being right here in this palace, isn't it?"

"Okay, everyone," came Louis's voice just as Kirsty was about to reply. "Let's move along to the Throne Room next."

The group followed him as he led the way out of the Jewel Chamber, and Kirsty and Rachel saw Caroline, another of the palace stewards, locking the door carefully once everyone had left the room. She put the keys in her pocket and hurried to catch up with the others.

The Throne Room was further along
the corridor. It was a huge room with
a high, vaulted ceiling, gilt-framed oil
paintings on the walls, and an enormous
red and gold patterned tapestry hanging
at one end. In front of the tapestry sat
two gleaming golden thrones studded
with jewels, with ornately carved arms
and backs.

"Oooh!" gasped some of the children,
and Kirsty and Rachel grinned at each
other in delight.
Both girls were thinking the same thing
– how the thrones reminded them of
King Oberon and Queen Titania's
thrones in Fairyland!

"Oh, I hope we meet another Princess
Fairy today," Rachel whispered to
Kirsty, and Kirsty nodded, feeling tingly

at the thought. Their fairy adventures were always so wonderful!

Louis invited the children to go up in pairs to try out the grand golden thrones. Rachel was surprised how small she felt, sitting on the large throne.

Kirsty, meanwhile, had to wait for a
boy wearing big trainers and a baseball
cap pulled low over his face, to get off
the throne.

"Come on, let
Kirsty sit there
now," Louis
called over,
noticing
Kirsty
waiting
patiently.
He smiled.
"I think someone is enjoying
being on a throne a bit
too much!"
The boy shuffled off reluctantly, and
Kirsty got to sit on the throne next to
Rachel. It was very cold and hard.

"The kings and queens would have needed cushions if they had to sit on these for very long," she giggled.

"Has everyone had a turn on the thrones? Wonderful," Louis said. "Our next stop is the Costume Gallery – where there's a surprise in store. This way!"

A Dress-Up
Mess-Up

Louis and Caroline led the children to
another room which had mannequins
dressed as kings, queens, knights,
servants, and musicians. There was even
a court jester mannequin, complete with
a red and yellow hat that had bells on
the end.

In the middle of the room stood a model of Golden Palace with tiny figurines positioned in the windows, dressed similarly to the mannequins.

Louis called everyone over to see the model, and pointed out the royal pageant that was taking place in the grounds. "A pageant, if you didn't know, means a display or a procession where people dress up to portray historical scenes," he explained.

"And that's what our surprise is," Caroline added. "Today, we're putting on our very own pageant right here at Golden Palace, which will be open to the public. And the stars of the show are going to be... all of you!"

Louis opened a cupboard door and pulled out a rail full of child-sized costumes. "Ta-dah!" he said.

Rachel and Kirsty smiled at one another in excitement. This sounded fun!

Other children were clamouring for the costumes they wanted. "Can I be a princess?" "Can I be a knight?" "Can I be the king?"

"Whoa," laughed Caroline, holding up a hand. "It's the luck of the draw." She produced an upturned jester's hat and showed them that it was full of slips of paper. "Take one of these and you'll discover who you're going to be for the pageant," she explained. One by one, the children took a slip and read it out.

"I'm a kitchen maid," laughed one boy.
"I'm a lute-player," read a girl. "I'm
the king!" said the youngest boy in the
group, looking thrilled — especially when
his big sister pulled out a slip saying that
she was the king's servant.

When the hat came to Rachel, she
took a slip which said, 'You are
a brave knight named
Sir Beaumont
who once helped
save this palace
from a deadly
enemy. He wore
a suit of armour
and carried a
sword.' "Cool,"
she said, passing
the hat to Kirsty.

"Sir Beaumont – he was the knight whose helmet we saw earlier, wasn't he? I like the sound of him."

Kirsty plunged her hand into the jester's hat… but it was empty. "Oh," she said in dismay. "I don't think there are any slips left."

Caroline took the hat from her and looked inside. "You're quite right," she said. "You must be the last one to pick your costume. Which means…" She turned the hat the right way up and plopped it on Kirsty's head. "…that you're our court jester!

Jesters had the very important job of
entertaining the royal family and
their guests."

Kirsty beamed.
"Thank you!"
she said, feeling
pleased.

Kirsty and
Rachel went
to find their
costumes. As
well as the rail of
outfits there was also a large box of
accessories, full of helmets, shoes, crowns,
armour and all sorts of other things.
Unfortunately, it soon became clear
that although each of the children could
find part of their costumes, there were
a number of things that were missing.

There were also items of clothing that didn't seem to belong there at all – like a witch's broomstick, an astronaut's helmet and a ballerina's tutu.

"This doesn't seem right," Louis said, looking puzzled as he held up some clown shoes and a robot costume. "I don't remember us having these before. Where are all our knights' swords?"

"We're just going to have to make do with what we've got," Caroline decided.

"Please do your best to put a costume
together, children. We'll come round and
help you."

Rachel had
a knight's
helmet but
no armour
or sword.
"Maybe this
robot costume
will do," she said
doubtfully. "It's silver, I suppose, so
looks a bit like armour." She rummaged
through a box of props. "I'll use this
broomstick as a sword."

Kirsty, meanwhile, had her hat but
no costume at all. "Jesters are funny,
aren't they," she reasoned, "so maybe
I should just wear something silly…"

She put on a ballet tutu and some
enormous clown shoes, then began
sorting through a smaller
box for something
she could use
instead of a
jester's stick. She
saw something
shining golden
in one corner
of the box and
reached further
down to feel
around. Was it a
golden bell on the end of
a jester's stick?

Something ticklishly light brushed
against her skin and she blinked in
surprise, then peered down into the box.

With a smile of delight she realised that
the golden sparkle she'd seen was coming
from a tiny smiling fairy, who was now
standing on the palm of her hand!

Carefully, making sure that nobody
else saw, Kirsty lifted the
fairy out of the box,
then took off her
jester hat and
popped the
fairy inside,
so that she
could stay
hidden. Then
she hurried to
a quiet corner
of the room and
beckoned Rachel
over to see.

"I've got some juggling balls," Rachel said, swinging them in a bag. "I thought they might be a good prop for you if you can't find... Oh!" Rachel broke off at the sight of the little fairy in Kirsty's hat. "Hello!" she said, beaming.

The fairy had long dark hair and was wearing a pink chiffon skirt and black-and-white striped top. Kirsty and Rachel had met all seven of the Princess Fairies the day before and recognised her as Princess Demi the Dressing-Up Fairy.

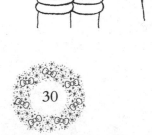

"Hello again," Princess Demi said in a high, silvery voice. She raised her eyebrows at the girls' costumes. "Looks like I got here just in time," she said. "Without my tiara full of dressing-up magic, this pageant – and theatrical events everywhere – will be a disaster!"

An Unusual Princess

"We'll help you find your tiara, Demi," Rachel said at once, and then her ears pricked up as she heard a loud, sulky voice coming from across the room.

"Where's my tiara? I can't be a princess without a tiara!"

The three friends looked over to see
a boy dressed in a pink frilly dress and
a long blonde wig. He was bending
over a box, rummaging through it so
that they couldn't see his face. Then
he straightened up and they heard him
mutter, "Well, if there's not a tiara here,
I know somewhere else I can get one..."

"What enormous feet that boy's got," Demi said suspiciously, pointing out the large trainers that poked out from the bottom of the pink dress.

"He's the boy who sat on the throne for ages earlier," Rachel realised. "What's he doing now?"

The three friends watched as the boy sidled nearer to Caroline. He waited until Caroline was distracted while adjusting somebody's helmet, then reached over and sneaked a hand into her pocket.

Kirsty and Rachel gasped as he drew out a bunch of keys and slunk away.

Just as he was leaving the room, they saw his face properly for the first time – and his skin was unmistakably green. He wasn't a boy at all – he was a goblin!

"Quick, let's follow him," Rachel said, and she and Kirsty hurried after the goblin, with Demi peeping out from Kirsty's jester hat.

The goblin had hitched up his dress and was scurrying down the corridor back towards the Jewel Chamber. Then they saw him take Caroline's keys, unlock the door and disappear inside.

"Oh no," Kirsty whispered in horror. "He's going to steal a real tiara from the jewel collection!"

"Wait," Demi said, as they approached the door of the chamber. "Let me turn you into fairies and we can all fly in there without him seeing us."

There was nobody in sight along the corridor so Kirsty and Rachel stood still while Demi waved her magic wand over them and muttered a few magical-sounding words under her breath.

Sparkles billowed around them and in the next moment, the two girls were shrinking smaller and smaller until they were the same size as Demi, and both had beautiful shimmering wings on their backs.

"Our costumes have shrunk too," Rachel giggled, seeing the now-tiny broomstick in her hand, and the bag of teeny juggling balls that Kirsty had slung over one shoulder. "Come in, let's see what he's up to."

The three fairies fluttered silently into
the Jewel Chamber, taking care to fly
high so that they weren't in the goblin's
line of sight. Then Demi's mouth
dropped open in surprise and she pointed
at the main display case. "Look!" she
hissed urgently. "It's
my magic tiara!"
Rachel
and Kirsty
gazed down
at the case.
Sure enough,
between a
glittering jewelled
necklace and a silver
bangle, was Demi's silver
jewelled tiara, gleaming and sparkling
against the black velvet background.

The fairies held their breath as the
goblin headed straight for this display
case and unlocked the door with another
of Caroline's keys. But before he could
grab the tiara, a second goblin burst into
the room. He was wearing a peaked cap
with 'Guard' written on it.

"Oi!" he
spluttered.
"Hands off!
Jack Frost
told me
to put the
tiara here
so that
it would
be safe
from those
meddling fairies.

I'm not allowed to let anyone near it, not even you."

The princess goblin stamped his foot. "Well, I'm playing Princess Goblina in the pageant, and I'm telling you, I *need* a tiara!"

The guard and princess goblins started arguing and while they were shouting at each other, Kirsty seized the chance to fly into the open display case. This was almost too easy, she thought, smiling. She could take the tiara from right under the goblins' noses!

But unfortunately, as she flew inside the case, the bag of juggling balls on her shoulder knocked the silver bangle off its hook, and sent it clinking to the floor.

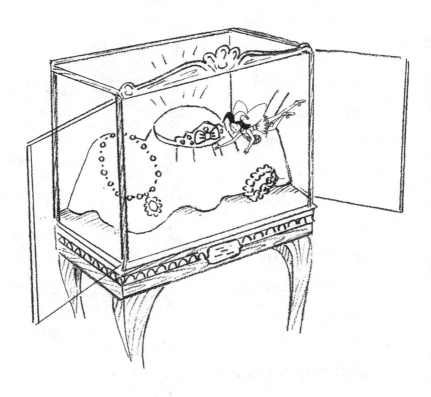

The goblins stopped arguing at once, and Kirsty froze in fright. The princess goblin's eyes gleamed when he saw Kirsty in the case and he snatched the tiara before she could even touch it. Then he slammed the door shut and locked it. Kirsty was trapped!

Sir Beaumont to the Rescue!

Rachel and Demi gazed helplessly at each other as Kirsty was locked behind the glass door. How could they get her out?

The guard goblin looked startled. He stared from Kirsty to the tiara back to Kirsty, as if he couldn't quite believe his eyes. "You see?" he shouted at the

princess goblin. "I *told* you to leave well alone. What if there are more fairies around, trying to steal our tiara?"

Demi gritted her teeth. "It's *my* tiara," she said in a tiny cross whisper.

"We need to find a better hiding place for it," the guard goblin went on. "Let me think…"

"How about on my head?" the princess goblin suggested, ramming it onto his blonde locks. "People will think it's part of my costume. Only *we'll* know that it's a real tiara."

The guard goblin looked doubtful. "Well… Oh, I suppose so," he said after a moment. "I can't think of anywhere better right now. But you've got to be careful with it, all right? Come on, let's get out of here before anyone spots us."

And with that, the two goblins left the room, Demi's tiara winking and glittering under the spotlights where it sat nestled in the goblin's wig. Demi and Rachel watched them go then flew down to Kirsty.

Rachel pulled at the glass door, hoping that the goblin, in his haste, might not have locked it properly, but it didn't move. "Are you all right in there?" she called through to her friend.

Kirsty nodded bravely. "I'm fine. Why don't you go after the goblins? We don't want to lose them."

Demi shook her head. "And leave you here, all alone? No chance!" she said. "A princess would never do such a thing. Now let's see if some good old fairy magic will open that glass door."

She pointed her
wand at the lock
and chanted a
complicated-
sounding spell
under her
breath. Nothing
happened.

Demi's shoulders
drooped. "Oh dear,"
she said. "Without my tiara, my magic
isn't as strong as it usually is. How can
we get you out, Kirsty?"

Rachel looked around for inspiration.
There had to be a way to set Kirsty free!
Then she caught sight of her costume
reflected in the glass door. Sir Beaumont
wouldn't have given up, would he? She
had to think of *something*…

She remembered the broomstick
she was holding. It wasn't exactly a
traditional weapon, but actually, now
that it had shrunk, it looked just the right
size to fit in the keyhole. "Maybe I could
use my broomstick to pick the lock," she
said eagerly. "Let me try…"

She pushed the end of the tiny
broomstick into the lock and jiggled it
a few times. To everyone's delight, the
lock clicked… and the
door swung open!
"Sir Beaumont
to the rescue,"
Rachel
laughed as
Kirsty flew
out and
hugged her.

"Thank you," Kirsty said happily.
"Now let's lock this case up again and
find those goblins!"

Demi flew down and replaced the
silver bangle, then Rachel shut the glass
door and used her broomstick to lock
it again.

The three fairies soared out of the
Jewel Chamber, closing the door behind
them. Then they flew down the corridor
in search of the goblins.

It wasn't hard to find them. The goblins were squabbling so loudly that it was easy to follow the sound of their voices. The three friends flew down a spiral stone staircase and into the Hall of Mirrors – a long rectangular room with mirrors of all shapes and sizes lining the walls. Princess Goblina was admiring the many different reflections of him wearing the tiara, while the guard goblin nagged at him to hurry up. "Come on, we need to go. Jack Frost trusted me to look after that tiara. He'll be furious if we don't find a safe place for it," he grumbled.

"Just wait," Princess Goblina snapped. "I've got to make sure it's on properly. Stop moaning!"

Rachel, Kirsty and Demi flew in quietly, staying close to the ceiling in

the hope that they wouldn't be spotted.
They knew that if Demi could just get
near enough to the princess goblin, she
could magic the tiara to fairy size and
take it back.

Unfortunately, before the fairies
could get any closer, the guard goblin
caught sight of their
reflections in one
of the mirrors.
His eyes
widened in
alarm and
he whirled
around.
"Fairies!"
he gasped.
"Run,
Goblina, run!"

Jest in Time!

The princess goblin pelted out of the room, one hand clutching the tiara protectively on his head, his trainers slapping against the tiled floor.

Kirsty, Rachel and Demi tried to fly after him but the guard goblin swatted at them with his big green hands. "Come here, you pesky creatures," he said, snatching at thin air as he tried and failed to grab them. "You're not getting that tiara — I won't let you!"

The fairies dodged and swerved around the guard's flailing hands, eventually managing to zoom out of the Hall of Mirrors and after the running princess goblin. They heard his loud footsteps go up the spiral staircase again… and then they went quiet.

"He's stopped," Demi said in surprise. "Unless he's taken his shoes off, maybe?" Kirsty suddenly remembered how much the goblin had enjoyed sitting on the throne earlier, and how she'd had to wait for him to get up.

"I wonder if he's gone back to the Throne Room?" she suggested.

The fairies flew along the corridor and peeked around the door of the Throne Room. Sure enough, the goblin was sitting on the throne once more, pretending to wave to a crowd of people.

"Good morning, everyone," they heard him say in a high-pitched voice. "Your princess is pleased to see so many admirers."

Rachel had to stuff a hand in her mouth to stop herself from giggling.

Kirsty looked thoughtful. "If we can keep him sitting there long enough, we might be able to fly above his head and get the tiara," she said. "But we'll need him to be distracted, so he wouldn't notice..."

Demi nodded. "Yes," she said. "What can we do to make sure he doesn't get off the throne?"

Kirsty reached up to scratch her head, forgetting for a moment that her jester's hat was there. Then she smiled. "I could be a jester," she said. "A real jester, entertaining Princess Goblina!"

A Perfect Pageant

Princess Goblina looked up in horror,
saw the fairies approaching and ducked
out of their way. But quick-thinking
Rachel remembered she still had her
trusty broomstick. Sir Beaumont – or
rather, Lady Rachel! – to the rescue
once again!

She lunged forward, stretching the broomstick out in front of her so that she could just reach the tiara with its end. Then she deftly flicked the tiara off the goblin's head, sending it flying through the air. She and Demi soared down, catching hold of it seconds before it clattered to the floor. As soon as Demi touched the tiara, it shrank to its usual fairy-size, and she was able to place it joyfully on her head.

"Hurrah!" she cheered, whizzing high in the air, with colourful sparkles of magic shooting out all around her. "Oh, that feels so much better!"

They whizzed through the air towards
Princess Goblina whose shoulders
were shaking with mirth. But at the
last moment, the guard goblin spotted
the fairies, and stopped
laughing abruptly.
"Goblina!" he yelled.
"Duck!"

Rachel flew up after her, and Kirsty beamed. The plan had worked perfectly!

The goblins meanwhile were arguing bitterly about whose fault it was that they'd lost the tiara, so Kirsty, Rachel and Demi slipped out of the Throne Room and left them bickering.

Outside, Demi waved her wand to turn Rachel back into her ordinary

size… and Rachel gasped when she
saw that she was now wearing the most
fantastic knight's costume ever! "Oh,
thank you, Demi!"

she said, beaming
as she flipped up
the visor on her
gleaming silver
helmet. "Even Sir
Beaumont would
be proud of this
outfit, I think."

"Thank *you*
so much," Demi
replied, smiling
happily. "Both of
you – you were amazing! I'm absolutely
thrilled to have my tiara back so that
I can use its dressing-up magic again.

Your pageant should turn out perfectly this afternoon."

"That's great news," Kirsty said. "I'm glad we could help you, Demi."

Demi gave each girl a tiny ticklish fairy kiss, then waved goodbye and disappeared in a swirl of sparkling magic. After the last sparkle had faded and vanished, the girls went to look for the other children.

They found them outside with Caroline and Louis on the main lawn in front of the palace. There was a tent serving refreshments, and rows of benches where the parents had gathered to watch.

"Look, there's Mum and Dad!" Kirsty said, waving and smiling at them in the audience. "Come on, let's ask Caroline what we're meant to be doing."

Just then a shout went up from Louis
as he saw a large box by the side of the
tent. "Hey, guys, I've
found the missing
dressing-up box,"
he said, a smile
spreading across
his face. "We've
got swords,
armour, kitchen
maids' outfits,
princess tiaras…
Now we can get you
all dressed up properly."
"Thank goodness," Caroline said,
helping Louis to give out the props and
costumes. "I wonder how that box got
down here? It's almost as if it appeared
by magic!"

She was laughing, but Kirsty and Rachel had spotted a few tell-tale sparkles twinkling on the box's side, and smiled at each other. Unknown to Caroline and Louis, Demi's magic really *had* saved the day. Now the girls could enjoy the pageant, and look forward to helping another fairy tomorrow!

Now it's time for Kirsty and
Rachel to help...

Anya the Cuddly Creatures Fairy

Read on for a sneak peek...

"Another perfect day!" said Rachel
Walker happily.

She was standing in the sunshine on the
grand entrance steps of Golden Palace.
Rachel's best friend Kirsty Tate looked
up and smiled as the bright sunbeams
warmed her face.

"It's royal weather for a royal palace!"
Kirsty agreed.

Kirsty and Rachel were staying at
Golden Palace for a special Kids' Week
over the spring holidays. Today, Kirsty's
mother was bringing Kirsty's little cousin
Charlie to spend the day with them.

"I'm looking forward to showing Charlie all the amazing places here," said Kirsty. "I wonder what he'll like best. The drawbridge? The moat?"

"Or the petting zoo, or the magic staircases, or the dungeons, or the maze," said Rachel, counting them off on her fingers. "There are so many things to show him, I don't think a day will be long enough!"

"Staying here really does make me feel like a princess," Kirsty said, gazing out across the palace gardens.

"How about a Princess Fairy?" Rachel asked.

The girls shared a secret smile. They were friends with the fairies who lived in Fairyland, and they often helped them when Jack Frost and his naughty

goblins caused trouble. At the moment, the fairies needed their help more than ever before. When the girls had arrived at Golden Palace, they had been invited to a special ball in Fairyland in honour of the Princess Fairies. But Jack Frost had gatecrashed the party and stolen the princesses' tiaras!

"Jack Frost is so mean," said Kirsty, thinking about the cold-hearted master of the Ice Castle...

Read Anya the Cuddly Creatures Fairy to find out what adventures are in store for Kirsty and Rachel!

Meet the Princess Fairies

Honor
the Happy Days
Fairy

Demi
the Dressing-Up
Fairy

Anya
the Cuddly Creatures
Fairy

Elisa
the Adventure
Fairy

Lizzie
the Sweet Treats
Fairy

Maddie
the Playtime
Fairy

Eva
the Enchanted Ball
Fairy

Jack Frost has stolen the Princess Fairies' special tiaras.
Kirsty and Rachel must get them back, or all the
magic in the world will fade away!

www.rainbowmagicbooks.co.uk

RAINBOW magic ®

Meet the fairies, play games
and get sneak peeks at
the latest books!

www.rainbowmagicbooks.co.uk

There's fairy fun for everyone on
our wonderful website.
You'll find great activities, competitions, stories and
fairy profiles, and also a special newsletter.

Get 30% off all Rainbow Magic books at
www.rainbowmagicbooks.co.uk

Enter the code RAINBOW at the checkout.
Offer ends 31 December 2012.

Offer valid in United Kingdom and Republic of Ireland only.

Competition

If you study this picture of the **Jewel Fairies** you'll see that one of the seven friends is missing! Can you work out who it is? Make a note of the first letter of the name of the missing fairy. When you have enjoyed all seven books in the Princess Fairies series, arrange the seven letters to make a special word, then send the answer in to us!

We will put all of the correct entries into a draw and select one winner to receive a special Rainbow Magic Princess Fairies Pack!

Enter online now at
www.rainbowmagicbooks.co.uk

Meet the
Pop Star Fairies

Jessie the Lyrics Fairy

Adele the Singing Coach Fairy

Miley the Stylist Fairy

Miley the Stylist Fairy

Twinkle the Make-up Fairy

Rochelle the Star Spotter Fairy

Una the Concert Fairy

Kirsty and Rachel have to save Rainspell Island Music Festival after Jack Frost steals the Pop Star Fairies' musical clef necklaces!

www.rainbowmagicbooks.co.uk

Afterglow